How I Became a Rock Star

A Memoir of a Musical Mind

SLATE MAGMA

ARCHWAY
PUBLISHING

Archway Publishing books may be ordered through booksellers or by contacting:

Archway Publishing
1663 Liberty Drive
Bloomington, IN 47403
www.archwaypublishing.com
844-669-3957

ISBN: 978-1-6657-1764-9 (sc)
ISBN: 978-1-6657-1765-6 (e)

Library of Congress Control Number: 2022900906

Print information available on the last page.

Archway Publishing rev. date: 1/27/2022

About The Author

Slate Magma's travels take you halfway around the world and all over this great country, the good ol' USA, on his journey to rock stardom.

When I first met this man in the first days of my army career, all he would talk about it seemed was music. Since I was a guitar player already, I was glad when he decided to pick up the bass. I wish our friend Durkin had kept playing, but, oh well.

Once he bought his first bass, he practiced all the time. We jammed all the time. Every spare moment the two of us had, we would play. Years went by till we got back together, and I couldn't believe what he had accomplished. I think you will enjoy his telling of his rise to Rock stardom.

SP5 Bullard (U. S. Army Ret.)

During the time I knew him, he loved music, so it didn't surprise me he went so far.

PFC Durkin (U.S. Army Ret.)

Let me tell you why I wrote this book.

I was at our family reunion the other day when my grandnephew asked me how I became a rock star. I told him it would take a little time, but I would love to tell him all about it. He said his brother wanted to know too, so I told him to go and get him. The two of them came in along with four of their cousins. I sat back and told them this story.

Slate Magma

Contents

How it all Started

It all started when I was twenty-two. I joined the army 'cause I was bored with life and needed a change.

You see I was just an average guy a few years out of high school. This job, and then that job, not sure what to do. My dad and all three of my uncles had been in the army, so I decided I would join. People often ask me if I was in a war back then, and I tell them "Yes, I was in the cold war."

The Army is a unique place in that everyone is different, I mean race, creed, character, intelligence, strength, gender, I mean every kind of difference, except my unit was male only, bummer.

At the in-processing station they called AAFES (Army Air Force Entrance Station) I picked out what sort of job in the army that I wanted, based on my aptitude tests. It would be some sort of mechanic. I chose a surface to air missile system. It was called a Chaparral. My second choice would have been a tank turret mechanic, which may have been the new M1-A1 Abrams tank. THE bad boy of tanks, but I'll never know 'cause I picked the Chaparral.

Chapparal

I raised my hand for the oath when I first signed on the dotted line on February twenty second. The oath that says I will defend the U.S. Constitution. I'm in, but I won't be going for three weeks. Three weeks later I raised my hand for the oath a second time and I was on my way.

The night before I left Chicago on that chilly march day I met my roommate in the military hotel, who was from Niles, Michigan. "Do you know Angelica Mills," I asked him?

"Yes, we used to date a couple of years ago," he told me.

"She's my cousin," I told him. We got a couple of six packs and hung in our room all night instead of hitting the local bars like most of the new enlistees. We got along fine, and my cousin years later told me he had mentioned that evening to her.

The next morning, I woke up at six fifteen, a little late and Bill was already gone. I never saw him again. Since I was running late, I only had time for a small breakfast and was starving all morning. I would tell you about the physical exams we all paraded thru but I'll save that for another story.

As most people know, the military in this country loves acronyms. I was learning that then. The guy on the loudspeaker kept saying "Attention in the MEPS." I later found out he had been announcing for a long time and MEPS was the old name, Military Entrance and Processing Station. Then it became AAFES, Army and Air Force Entrance Station, which is what all my paperwork called it. I have no idea what they call it these days, all these years later, but it was confusing then. After the final swearing in session, it was off to O'Hare International Airport.

For the trip to basic training, I was selected the leader of the four of us and they said it was my responsibility that all four of us met Army personnel at the El Paso airport. Henry Scott, Bill Broadrick, Bryant Herdt and I were on our way. We left O'Hare airport shortly after three pm. The food on that flight was good but not enough. I was still hungry around seven that evening when we touched down at DFW International. How cool is that. It was freezing back home and now it's seventy-five degrees.

Now, we had a two and a half hour wait for the flight to El Paso. We went where all young men (except Scott was twenty-nine, you know, old) would go to kill time. Let's find beer. I thought about a burger or something, but airport food was way too expensive. I didn't have much money, so beer it was. We drank two or three beers each during our wait till they called our flight and we boarded right away. Man, how things change, huh? The only problem was we had to go down some stairs, outside and up the stairs to the back door of the plane. I found out later why. They said the latch on the regular door was under repair and would be finished soon. This route would speed things up. They were right and in ten minutes, or so we were moving. The flight wasn't quite long enough for a meal, so I still hadn't eaten enough. Man, *I'm hungry*. As we were finding our seats the stewardess said a mistake was made with the seating and the seats were over sold. She said one of us would have to fly in the first-class section. We agreed three to one who should get the good seat and I lost. I didn't want anything fancy, but it's good to be the boss. First class seats are nice, and I got a free beer too, although at that altitude it just put me to sleep. At the airport in El Paso, I was still groggy from the beer and sleep, but we met the Army personnel anyway and they whisked us away and on to Fort Bliss. Mission accomplished.

The bunk beds we were given were along a wall, head to foot about two feet apart. There were a couple of guys awake but they didn't look happy about it, but they showed us to our bunks. "Put your bags there and get in that bunk and go to sleep" they were barking oh so quietly. All I was able to do that late at night with the flights and all was to obey. Goodnight.

2

Into the Uknown

After the late flight the night before, one a.m. arrival and a six o'clock wake up, they got us outside and in line and started teaching us how to march. Thankfully they marched us to the mess hall first. Man, *I'm hungry.*

Mess Hall

Outside the mess hall we had to line up, front to back, at attention and moving forward into the mess hall five people at a time.

Five, would come the bark from inside. If we didn't snap to attention and step forward, we would get yelled at.

After breakfast we went to get our uniforms, unders, tee's, socks and the like. After we got all of that, we put our civilian clothes, *civvies* into boxes and they were locked away.

While we were standing around, and we did it a lot, I met this guy with a full beard, mustache, and obviously a huge head of hair down to his shoulders and beyond. He said his name was Wilkins and I told him mine. We talked that morning and once again that early afternoon.

The next morning after morning chow we went back to the same place to get more gear. I met a guy with no beard and a big cheesy mustache and long hair, so I introduced myself and he says, "It's me Wilkins, we met yesterday."

"Wilkins you look so diff..." it was hard to finish since we were laughing so much. He said he was taking it off a step at a time.

The next day was barber day and before we went to get the shaved hair cut that all seventy-five or so of us got, and the shortest cut I've ever had, I saw Wilkins again with no mustache, and when I said, "Hi, I'm..."

He stopped me, and said, "don't do this again."

I said something like "I remember this time, oops." People can look so different.

The next time we needed haircuts I had already met my new friend Bullard. Him and I and a few of the other guys got shaved again just for fun. We called ourselves the *coz* team, but I can't remember why.

After we got to know each other better, and our hair started to grow back a little, I learned that Bullard was a guitar player. I thought that was cool because I had learned to play a little back in seventh grade, but he said he left it all at home till training was over. During basic training it was all soldier stuff and nothing about our other interests.

Right Face

We weren't allowed radios or cameras or anything, but I managed to sneak in a camera and a transistor radio with an earplug. I still can't believe I never got caught with them. During my fireguard shifts (one hour a night) I used to listen to the local radio. I also got some good pictures of basic training that I don't think anyone else was able to get. Otherwise, it was nothing but training.

We even had a new recruit and his wife sent him a joint in the mail. For those of you who don't know, a joint is a marijuana cigarette. He was singled out and, no, he didn't get the joint, but he did have to do some *extra duty*. That's after hours work while I'll be reading my mail or having a smoke, a regular smoke. I still wonder what happened to that joint. Did the drill sergeants keep it or through it away? They did seem happier the next day. I wonder.

During the first two days of basic training, after in processing, when we were all lined up and in formation, they would tell us that when they call out our number we would sound off with our name. When they called Scott's number he would say "Scott," when they called my number, I said my last name with conviction. But when they called Heardt's number he would say in his high squeaky voice, "Heardt."

The drill sergeant would bark "I SAID YOUR NAME, NOT HERE".

It took two days before they realized his name sounded like *here*.

Charlie Battery

After we got out of basic training, we went to the school brigade. That's where we received our mechanical and electronics training. That's where it really started. Kaufman really opened my eyes. He started playing guitar at the beginning of the School Brigade. He hardly went out in the evenings, instead, staying in to learn. He had books and cassette tapes and taught himself to play. It was only two guys to a room and his roommate liked to go out in the evenings, so Kaufman had the room mostly to him self. That's much better than the thirty or so in bunks in the barracks during basic.

Three months later, after School Brigade and at Ft. Hood, Kaufman became second chair guitar in the 2ⁿᵈ Armored Brigade band. Music was important at that time because we finally were allowed to listen to the radio or a turntable or cassettes, no cd's back then. We also had small refrigerators in our rooms and a TV in the day room that had a beer machine. That's the common room everybody shared.

No one else had any actual instruments except Kaufman's guitar stuff. Bullard did help Kaufman at the beginning, but he soon caught up to Bullard, and in my opinion, he learned quick and got better. That's when Kaufman told Bullard about these rooms in an army building that he had found that are very soundproof. Bullard rented a guitar and the two of them jammed a few times.

After basic and advanced individual training, AIT (still in the same barracks as basic), and the School Brigade we went to Fort Hood, Texas.

Kaufman, Olsen and some others went to the 2nd Armored Division and Bullard, Durkin and some of us went to the 1st Cavalry Division. Both part of 3 Corp, Ft Hood, Texas. Other guys went everywhere from Fort Carson, Colorado to Korea. Olsen and I both put Korea on our wish list 'cause we figured they wouldn't send us where we wanted to go. And you know, it worked.

The 2nd Armor guys were about three miles north of us and there was a bus that went back and forth from the CAV area and downtown, right by 2nd Armour. I didn't know it at the time, but Bullard had gone home during our leave time between basic/AIT /School, and our regular duty and he had picked up his guitar and amp and brought it with him. So as soon as we got our rooms and had time to move in, Bullard was playing in his room. I was thinking, hearing it from next door, that it would be stopped instantly, you know, too loud. He played for about twenty minutes before he stopped.

Then the knocks came. Listening from next door I heard a commotion. *Oh No*, I thought, *Bullard is in trouble only an hour after he moves in.* But then he starts playing again. I had to go check it out. This place is cool, I was thinking, and then I heard the music down the hall. Country Music, kind of loud, cool, my thoughts.

Now Bullard and I were in the 1st Battalion, 68th Air Defense Artillery 1st Cavalry Division, or 1/68th ADA 1CD.

We were in Delta Battery, Headquarters Platoon. I was in squad A and Bullard was in squad C. This friend of Bullard's from basic that I only knew briefly named Durkin was in Charlie Battery, just downstairs from us. It turned out that one of Durkin's desires out of the army was to learn the guitar. He had saved some cash to buy equipment, you know, you gotta get loud. So, Bullard and Durkin started jammin'. I had no way to join in since I really didn't know how to play either, since my seventh-grade attempt wasn't that good. As Durkin kind of started learning to play, his wife kept saying he was no good. *Ben*, she said many times, *You're much better as a dad than a guitar player, you're better at a lot of things than a guitar player. But Honey, I love the guitar*, his usual response. But he and Bullard kept practicing.

When I was in seventh grade, I learned the basics of the six-string guitar and how to finger pick, but I soon grew bored with that as most seventh graders loose interest in one thing or another. Even in the first-grade music was instilled in my brain and there were instruments shown to me. First grade with Glee Club, third grade with horn and reed instruments, and fifth grade with strings like the cello which I loved the sound of, and violin. By the way, my oldest sister plays the violin... sorry, the *viola*, and a few years later I used to watch her quartet jams. Those days were so cool, and the cello was my favorite. So, when Bullard suggested I think about learning bass guitar I was intrigued.

I went to a local pawnshop and bought a used bass guitar. I then had to save for an amplifier, and I had to learn how to play bass. I bought a couple of books by Mel somebody that taught bass guitar and started practicing every night in my barracks room. I couldn't hear very well without an amp, but I still worked my fingers all over those scales. My roommates didn't like the noise I was making, clunk, clunk, twang et cetera, so I moved my learning space to Durkin's apartment where he lived with his wife. He had a stereo that I could plug my bass and headphones into and play along with what ever songs I wanted to. I'm so glad for the Durkin's.

So, it took a couple of months to pull it all together, but eventually we started a band. Bullard and Durkin and myself. *what a trio*, we thought. A month later during a break in practice, Durkin asked, "what do we call our selves?"

"How 'bout The Three Inmates," I asked in jest. We never did come up with a name. We jammed for about three months or so when Durkin said he (and his wife) decided he wasn't cut out to be a guitar player. WOW what a bummer for us, but Bullard and I decided to keep playing anyway. We tried jammin' with a couple of different guys, but they were all no-gos.

Being in the army you have access to lots of fun stuff. We had access to these great little rooms, like at the School Brigade, the kind Kaufman told Bullard about, they were here too, soundproof rooms, the kind you can crank it up inside, but you can't hear anything outside, yea, *we have them here too*, I would think with a grin. Well, we spent three or four hours every Saturday in those soundproof rooms.

There was one guy named Searle who said he was a drummer in his high school marching band. Bullard and I decided we should get him to play drums for us. That was a mistake it seems, now looking back. Almost every time he would aim at the hi-hat, he would miss and knock over a ride. Every time he would hit the cymbal right next to the snare, he would knock over some other ride. CRASH. "All right let's start over," Bullard would say, growing more impatient every time. We had to cut Searle off.

Then there was Spence. He was a strummer extraordinaire in his own right. He didn't need to play lead 'cause his chord style was lead enough. He was only with us at Ft. Hood for about three months or so and we really didn't have time to jam properly.

I really think his wife was jealous of us. She would hang outside of the jam rooms and sometimes she would just stay outside. She was so lonely when he was ignoring her for fifteen minutes of jammin', that she even cried once. She was so cute, and Spence really loved her, but Spence loved the guitar too. I miss his guitar sound. Spence are you out there?

Eventually Bullard and I got sent to Germany for war games for about a month and a half. It was called REFORGER. That stands for *Return of Forces to Germany.* Let's get ready for WWIII.

As soon as we got to the first army base in Germany that we stayed at, we looked for those little rooms we loved back state side. We found them and to our surprise, they had brand new guitars and basses there, and it was my birthday, twenty-four.

We were there for five days and spent four sessions of about two hours each in those loud fun jammin' rooms. I think I learned more with those new basses than I did playing my used pawnshop beater. That's the only jammin' we got to do during that time period, though. I was messing around a little bit with harmonicas at that time too, so at least I had something to jam with.

After we got back state side, I knew I had to buy a good bass guitar. I looked at the pawnshops around the area, and as with all military towns, there are all kinds of pawnshops. I found some really nice basses but nothing I could afford, or thought was worth the price, and besides, I had no cash and no real credit to speak of. I had bought a four-year-old car from a dealership back home three years before. That was it as far as credit and it didn't get me anywhere. So, I bought a cheap bass and a cheap beat-up amp from a pawnshop. The guitar only lasted about four months. We were playing and everything was good for a while. Then, next thing you know, I started sounding flatter and flatter till I looked at the neck. It looked like a gooseneck, all twisted.

So, three days later I went to one of those stores that sells everything a G.I. could ever need and give you credit. I found a nice brand-new bass (I still have all the pieces). It was a Fender copy. As I learned with playing more different basses, it was a pretty good cheap bass. I paid one hundred and fifty dollars for that guitar and man it played great. I learned real soon that a guitar player must tune more often than a bass player. He also needs to change strings more often. I liked that thought cause bass strings were about twenty bucks a set and lasted almost forever and Bullard had to change his five-dollar set of strings every couple of weeks or so, usually sooner.

Every Friday afternoon when the weekend started, I would walk down the hallway in my barracks with my bass strapped around my neck and amp in hand, (man this is heavy, and there were no gig bags back then) I would go downtown to Durkin's place and jam with Durkin and Bullard. It seemed like every Friday someone in the hallway would ask, *where yall playing tonight*, and I would tell him, *a big club in Austin* or *some stadium in Dallas* or somewhere. It was a big joke after a while. All the while thinking maybe someday it would actually come true.

Barracks Hall

I do remember some guy, one of the rap music guys in the barracks, wanted to learn the bass, so after I was on book two of my learning tool books, I gave him book one. I showed him how the book worked and all of that, but I don't know if he learned to play or not, but his music style and mine were very different. A couple of other guys showed some interest too, but he was the only one I helped at all.

I do remember Sgt Faulkenbush, who was a good guitar player, showed up in the barracks. He and Bullard automatically hit it off and soon the three of us were jammin'. I was getting pretty good myself after such a short time. Maybe I've got something going here.

It was New Year's Eve at about one 1 pm that day when we started playing and about six, we stopped for evening chow. We then stopped at about 10 pm to get some beer. We played till about three in the morning until the CQ (that's the guy in charge of the quarters over night) said it's late enough and we should quit. I told him I'll never quit playing but I'll stop for the night. Get it?

After about three or four weeks of practice, we had enough songs to play a forty-five-minute set. Perfect, we thought. We asked around town like all the other bands, but Bullard talked to just the right guy and guess what? We've got a gig. Then I thought, *we've no drums.* Oh well, we'll just play our best and have fun.

We played at this little bar, or club called Frederick's Favorite Inn a few times, two guitars and a bass. Bullard would sing. He even came prepared with his own mic. We were pretty good but still kind of raw, and no drummer. The club was only about ten feet wide by about twenty-five feet long with glass and mirrors everywhere. It was a good thing we only had small amps 'cause the sound in that little place was terrible.

The first two times, there were only ten or twelve people there, but by the fifth time we played for around twenty. "Cool, we almost doubled our audience," I said to Bullard.

"Yes, let's triple it next time," Bullard responded. The last night there we actually made twenty bucks a piece. We played some Stones, which I can't stand hearing, BTO, Ten Years After, and some other late sixties and early seventies songs. Man, this is fun.

Then the bass player from a band called *Safety Net* that played regularly in Austin came up to me afterwards and said he thought we were pretty good but really needed more. That was when we knew that we needed a drummer, big amps and all that loud stuff.

Then we met this new guy named Claiborne, a good drummer who, like us, joined the Army to do something new. He said he wanted to see the world. The funny thing is he was from Oatmeal, Texas, not all that far from Fort Hood. He had just come into Alpha Battery around the corner from our barracks. He was glad for those little rooms cause there was no way he could play drums in the barracks, way too loud, don't you know. We practiced with him for a couple of days while bringing him into the final gigs at Fredericks.

Claiborne said his dad was a guitar player, so he naturally had to get into music. He told me he always loved the music, but it was the beat that kept him going. I explained that it was the beat for me also, but I had to have the low end of the music to hold. By this time, we were able to *rent*, even though it was free since it was army property, not just those *rooms*, but also an actual stage. A movie theater turned into a sound studio building and we got the stage. How cool is that at twenty-three years old.

We played at four clubs around town a total of sixteen times with Clayborne, but my favorite time was at The Millionaires Club. There were no bars in that county. They all had to be *clubs*. The big difference between a bar and a club is at a club you become a member. It only costs a dollar or two but it's good for a month. Anyway…the Millionaires Club was about sixteen hundred square feet of tin roof over air-conditioned concrete block stuffed with a hundred or so partiers. We played there eight times. The other gigs before Claiborne were good but Claiborne really stepped us up. Now when we jam at the Millionaires, we ROCK. For some reason when we played at the Millionaires Club, we were just so tight. We really rocked. Can I say that again? We were good those nights. After some more time (weeks) we had two and a half sets of forty-five minutes each, enough for a whole night's show.

One place we played was a little club called Big Horn's Little Place. No kidding. We showed up around six o'clock and set everything up in a half hour or so. After we set up, we went to get chow, but not in the mess hall, but at a really good greasy burger place. Man was it good. I hadn't had a good greasy burger since before joining. While we were eating, some guy comes in and says that some trashy band is playing tonight at Big Horns. "Hey," I said to him, "how do you know they're trashy if you've never heard them?"

"Stuff I heard, aren't all of these army bands crap," was his only response.

So, I gave him one of our few passes we were allowed to give out and said, "Just give us a listen."

He said, "you're in this crappy band?"

"Yes, I'm the bass player in this *not* crappy band and how can you judge us if you've never heard us before." He left and said he'll be there.

When the show started, I was delighted to see us under a few colored lights over the stage. After the first song the small but enthusiastic crowd bellowed and cheered. That guy from the burger place was clapping and smiling. It was awe-inspiring. I'll never quit playing, well, at least maybe just for the night.

Five minutes after the show, that guy came backstage and apologized and said we sounded *totally awesome*, and apologized again for his comments before hand.

The really cool thing about ending a gig is the people that come over to talk to us afterwards. I do recall after one show, a sweet young brunette came back to hit on Bullard and a blonde one hit on me. But that's another story.

At the millionaire's club, we had to set up around four pm. This place had a bigger stage, by far, than the old stage on base. This stage was huge. They had sound guys there to wire everything. It took a lot of time to get the sound just right. By seven-thirty or so that evening we finally got to eat. *Man, I'm hungry.* We came back around eight-thirty and went on stage at nine. *This is the big time*, my thoughts were reeling in my head, *I can't wait to hear the recording of it*. But during it, we rocked. We did a killer version of Clapton's "Layla". We ended with ZZ Tops "Heard It on the X". We only played there those few times, but it was so awesome, to be cheered like that.

Then Faulkenbush somehow booked a gig in Waco. We walked into the bar (a different county and no clubs) and were immediately patted down for weapons. "We're the band for crying out loud," Faulkenbush barked quietly. It was a pretty weird night because we were all white and the cop at the door and all of the bar's help were white, but all of the customers were black. It turned out to be no big deal because they loved us. We only played there once but I went back there one more time just to drink. I don't remember the name of that bar, but I met some really cool people.

That gig in Waco got us another gig at a really, big nightclub in Waco. Not just a bar, but also a place with six separate bars and three mechanical bulls. *Billie's Big Time*, the biggest nightclub in Waco was the place. Each dance floor was as big or bigger than the whole building on base where we used those little rooms and the stage. All we needed to bring was our axes (guitars) and our amps and drums. They had everything else to crank up the volume. They had power amps, speakers, lights, and everything.

We left Fort Hood at about eight that Saturday morning and drove to Waco. We borrowed a van from Sergeant Wexler to haul our stuff and got to town two hours or so later. On the way we were on U.S. 35 and witnessed a car we had passed where the people in the car were passing a joint around. The car swerved and the driver lost control and a truck t-boned it. Later I read about it in the paper and fortunately everyone was okay. Please leave that stuff at home when you are highway driving.

The nightclub was still closed when we got there so we found a cool little restaurant for lunch and pigged out. Now we had hours too kill. "I told you guys we didn't have to leave so early," I complained, We found something fun to kill the time, though. Waco had a really cool zoo, so we hung out there till around five. Then we went to a really nice restaurant for dinner. I had the best steak I'd had in years. Army steaks are really tuff and chewy, but this one was so good.

Finally, we arrived at the nightclub. They chewed us out for being late and said we should have been there an hour earlier. "Bullard, you said seven, not six."

"Sorry," was all he could say. No big deal we were told, let's get going. We hadn't even finished our two-song sound check when they opened the doors to the public. This place was so big I was nervous as could be. Bullard played cool but I could tell he was nervous too. Claiborne and Faulkenbush both seemed a nervous wreck also. The crowd was anxious and yelling and everything till we started playing and then they all went silent. I got worried until they all together seemed to erupt into a cheer all together. WOW what a night. We played for four hours that night and I made enough money to buy a brand-new Warwick bass. That was the coolest night of my life. They told us there were over four hundred people there. I wanted every Saturday night to be the same as that night.

We played there one more time with even a bigger crowd. Maybe you heard of us if you were in Waco around that time, *The Rockin' Rangers*. On our way home to Fort Hood after the second night, still in Sergeant Wexler's van we got pulled over for expired plates. I tried to explain to the officer that it wasn't my van and that I borrowed it from a fellow soldier at Fort Hood, but I got a ticket anyway. We spent two hours at a little police station at some little town between Waco and home. That kind of ruined the night, but not too much.

While that was all happening, I was also becoming a short timer. That's a guy who is counting down his days till he gets out of the army. I was down to around thirty days or so. It was the same thing with Bullard since we joined the same day. We told the guys back in the barracks that we were headed for the big time, but we knew it was ending.

Oh yeah, I almost forgot about the '61 Fender Statocaster I owned for about a month. I bought a pawn ticket from an eltee (Lieutenant) and got out that Strat, which had floated around hands in my battalion for a while. I then lost it back in the same pawnshop four weeks later. Probably the dumbest rock (and financial) moves I ever made. It probably would be worth twenty or thirty thousand dollars now. Oh well.

As the time came to an end, we wished each other good luck and farewell, and let's try and keep in touch. That was the last Bullard and I talked for ten years till I tracked him down exactly ten years to the day that we were released from the army. He told me he was actively playing in bands and doing ok. I told him about my current band stuff and how it all was, but I'm not letting on yet here. By the time my three years were up and time to hed home back to the Chicago area, I had bought a two hundred watt brand new amp head and a new small forty-watt bass combo. Now my rock world was on hold, for a while.

Well, that's the way it happened in Texas, all one thousand ninety-three days worth. That's my story and I'm sticking with it! Time to go home.

On my way home, my backseat and half of the front seat were filled with my clothes and guitars and the like, the car was full. I only had room otherwise for me. The trunk held most of my amps and guitar stuff. I took two and a half days to drive home 'cause I really had nothing to go home to, so I took my time.

Once I got home, I applied for unemployment since I was out of, work but the state said I didn't qualify. "OK, how do I eat, and where do I live?" I asked. I was told that since I left on my own, I wouldn't qualify for three more weeks. Oh well, I guess it's back to the folk's house till I get settled.

Moving On

After a couple of months working at a local gas station, I found a job as a mechanic at a small rental yard. I started on a Tuesday and the manager, Rob, said, "You should meet Tinley Steel, he's a part time driver who works on Monday's. He's a guitar player."

"That's cool," I told him, "I need to find some rockers to jam with."

That next Monday, Tinley was there, and Rob introduced us. We got along fine that day and one week later, Tin, as I started calling him, told me about his friend Rock Hampton. I wasn't sure about either name, but Tin said his was real, but Rock was a nickname. Two weeks later I met Rock. Rock was a strummer and very good at it and Tin was working on his lead stuff. I found out as time went on that Tin was a strummer but really wanted to learn leads. *Oh no, a new guy*, I thought. Fortunately, I was wrong, and he only needed a little more time.

Tin and Rock were so excited cause they had been jammin' for a couple of weeks with no drummer and no bass player. Tin, he later told me, told Rock, "I met a bass player from Texas, now we can really jam." It took a couple of tries, but I finally convinced them that I was only in Texas for three years, and I was really from four miles south, you know, your high school rivalry. They both said they really didn't follow high school sports and didn't know much about my hometown, and I guess I had picked up a little southern accent after three years in Texas, though. We still laugh about that all these years later.

Since I was the mechanic in that rental yard, I had a key and the bosses lived miles away, we started jamming' there twice a week. I lived in an apartment across the commuter tracks, which I could see from work. The sound inside was good, and we could jam on our own terms. *Cool, like those little rooms, but bigger,* I thought.

Rob, the store manager, it turned out, had a really good voice, so every now and then he would come to the jams and sing, so that was fun.

Tin and Rock were kind of related because a year or so after they met, Rock married Tin's sister and the singer who joined us was Tin's wife's brother, John, and they all worked together. They were all family and I, well; I was just the bass player. But, without me, they couldn't quite do it alone. But it's all teamwork, you know.

Tin was a strummer who was hell bent on getting the lead end of things working. Him and I worked on that for months and he always improved, as was my bass playing. *things couldn't be better,* I thought.

John had a cousin who played drums. He went by the name of Spike, which fit since he was pretty good, but for some reason was just too crazy, you know, too fast. Way too fast for his ability, and our style. After all we were all in our late twenties or so, but we liked a more subtle acoustic sound.

Rock is four or five years older than I am and Tin is a year younger than me. John, it turned out is only one day older than I am, and Spike and I went to high school together. One day just a week or so after Spike joined us, he asked me what my last name was, and I nonchalantly told him "Bassman."

He said, "that's so cool." but I had to tell him I was just joking and asked him about high school. That's when he and I remembered each other from that time.

John, it turned out, found us a gig in Waukegan at a waterfront *taste of* type carnival party week. We thought that that would be our ticket on the road to stardom. As it turned out, the whole music end of it was a wash out 'cause they ran out of money to pay all the bands

All five of us talked about it the next day and we agreed we would play for free. We need to get our name out there, some how. So, John called the folks in charge and told them our decision and they said we could play. A couple of other corny (in my view) music acts also performed for free.

By this time, I was working for a ski and patio store (skiing stuff in the winter and patio furniture stuff in the summer) and it was time for pre-winter (august) ski tech clinics.

The afternoon before the gig in Waukegan, myself and the other technicians at the ski shop went to the clinic and our boss, who knew the technical editor for SkiStuff magazine stayed afterwards to have a few drinks with us guys, and we stayed late drinking. The next day, the morning of the gig, I think we went on stage around three that afternoon, I mentioned to Rock that I was hung over just a bit. Rock asked, "Are you ok to play."

"Of course," I told him, "I'm a pro, let's go jam."

One fun thing we did to prepare for that gig was to make some t-shirts with our band name on them for the family kids to wear. I put one on under my shirt so that during breaks I could advertise us but for some reason, the guys shunned me. "Those are supposed to be for the kids." I was told.

"What," I asked, "we can't wear them too?" They ignored me so I guess I was right. I had told three or four of my work friends about the gig and to my surprise, they showed up with about twenty or so adults and kids combined. We still have the video tape from that gig.

After the show, some heavy set, sweaty guy came up to John and I and said he was with the local musician's union, and we *must* join. John started to tell him a thing or two, you know, get in his face. I jumped in and told the guy to give me his card and that I would be in touch. He was fine with that, but I never called him. We don't need no stinkin' union.

One other fun thing during that gig was the bubble machine. We did a song with Tin's son who was about six or seven years old then. They turned on the bubble machine during that song. The ladies in the crowd loved the effects and the kid singing. After we got back home from the gig, we all met at Tin's house to watch the video, except for Spike. We were all so drained from the experience that we just sat there staring at the TV. Three days later Spike asked to borrow the tape so he could watch it.

After a couple of more practice nights, Spike showed up with some cocaine. After about an hour or so he said he was too hot to play and needed a break. *okay* we all agreed, *let's take five or so.* He took off all his clothes except his unders and went outside. "That's pretty weird," Rock said.

"No kidding," was Tin's and my response.

I told them, "Spike and I went to dinner a couple of weeks ago and afterwards, hanging at my place, he went into the bathroom and ten or fifteen minutes later, he did the same thing. He was gone for about a half hour. As soon as he got back, he got dressed and went home, but I didn't know about any cocaine."

Later that month I went to see Neil Young at an outdoor concert with some of us guys. The place was about thirty miles away from home and halfway through the show Spike just up and left. He didn't drive there so no one knew what happened to him. "John, go have him paged," I said after the show. He did and they did, but Spike was nowhere to be found. We later found out he had taken a cab home. That must have cost him fifty bucks or more. We decided he could no longer represent our band as the drummer. Now we had to find us a new drummer.

A couple of years later, Rock surprised us with that tape Spike had borrowed from the gig in Waukegan that we thought was gone forever. Thanks for small miracles. Rock had run into Spike somewhere and he returned the tape to Rock. "Sorry for keeping it and all the trouble I gave you," Spike told Rock. "I got married and gave up the coke and the drums."

Well, that was good news, we all agreed. Shortly after that John got married and decided he was done singing. *Bummer*, Tin, Rock and I agreed.

During this time, my boss at the ski shop, who was a guitar player, asked me if I wanted to play with him and his old buddy, Wilmignton. Wilmington Harvardstone, and he didn't want to be called Will, had just bought a new full drum set. He seemed to me to be a cool guy, but somewhat wealthy. He had learned to play in junior high school, but he hadn't played since. "Sure, I'll come by and see how it goes." Well, we played a few times, but it wasn't anything *bandable*, but it was always fun.

It turned out to be a decade long jam session, maybe twelve years. I was really lucky knowing Wilmington 'cause he invited all sorts of guitar players over, and I was the house bass player, so to speak. Every couple of months or so I got to play with different guitar guys and man it was fun. Since *Diminished*, as Tin, Rock and myself called ourselves, practiced twice a week, and once a week at Wilmington's, I was very busy. I had to practice regularly on my own with our homegrown stuff as well as classic's over at Wilmington's place; I was busy five nights a week. I didn't mind cause rock 'n' roll was my life.

Rock found a new drummer to replace Spike, and he had a basement to play in like Wilmington's. WOW, what a relief. Now we can try to get more gigs. Bill Webster, Thriller Bill, as he liked to be called, had a place we could really crank it up in. Home grown music, Neil Young, CSN, and lots of other music were played good and, uh loud.

Rock had started singing after John left and we all, family and friends alike, agreed that he should sing out front. "Tin and I'll sing back up, but you should sing lead," Tin told him.

Tin started pressing, "Now we can get more gigs."

"I agree," I said many times.

I remembered a bar I went to before I was in the army that had bands and I mentioned it to the guys. Tin right away said, "Well, go get us some gigs."

"You betcha," I responded. The next day I called Sueby's Tavern and talked to Cecil B. DeNeglo, or Cecil B. as he was known. You know, like DeNiro! He was one of the main bartenders I knew and surprisingly enough to me he was still working there.

"Cecil, I don't know if you remember me from a few years ago," I asked?

"Of, course I do, what's up buddy," he said.

"I'm in a really good band and we're looking to find some work, are you still having bands play on Saturday nights?"

"Yes, we are, can you bring me a demo tape. Oh, by the way. I didn't know you played," he asked.

"Yes, I can and yes I do," I told him.

Well, now we had a problem. How do we record a good demo tape? We went to Radio Shack and bought a cassette recorder we could plug mics into and a couple of cheap mics. Two weeks later we finally had three songs recorded good enough for my taste to give to Cecil.

I went to Sueby's and met with Cecil. He told me he was just leaving work right then for a couple of hours and would I come with him back to his place. He had a good stereo there and some good steaks waiting for us, his treat. "Sure Cecil, let's go, man I'm hungry," I eagerly told him.

When we got to his place, he introduced me to his wife Jill. She said the steaks would be ready in about twenty minutes. We went down to the basement bar and put the tape in. I said, "don't expect much from the recording quality, but our sound should impress you."

He listened for about twenty seconds and reached for the volume control. My first thought when I saw him reach was, *he was turning it off*, but to my surprise, he cranked it up. Then he started playing air guitar, which cracked me up. Jill came running down the stairs to hear. She looked at me and asked, "is this your band, this is really good?" Then she started the air guitar stuff too.

We listened and played air guitar for a couple of songs when Jill yelled, "the steaks," and ran upstairs. After we ate, and Jill was so good at cooking those steaks, we went back to the bar and Jill came with.

Once in the bar Cecil asked me if I wanted to let the patrons at the bar decide if they liked our music. It seemed to me like we were a go for playing there, but I still wasn't sure. "Sure, put it on," I said.

So, he got on the PA and said, "Here's a new band for you," and played the tape for the entire bar to hear.

At first no one said anything but after the first song there were some cheers, but not that much. After song two, the audience was more into it. After the tape ended almost all the twenty-five or so patrons cheered and yelled together "Who's The Band, Who's The Band?"

Cecil went to the intercom. "Who would like this band to play here this Saturday night?" The bar erupted with cheers. As you can guess, we played there that Saturday night and many more after that. Thank you, my old friend Cecil.

Sueby's is a fun place five miles south of the town where we practiced at, so it was nice and close to gig at. At the first gig at Sueby's I was pleased to see a bunch of people I knew in high school. There was John Favorite, Bill Hill and Frank Foukel to name a few. Bob Moran was there too. I remember in high school, we used to sing, Bob Bob Bob Bob Bob Moran. Just like the old *Barbara Ann* song. He didn't like that very much, but I digress.

John Favorite was all hyped up in the fact that I was in a band. "Wow," he told me, "I never knew you could rock like that."

"Thanks, and it's good to see you too. Come back next week

and we'll rock out again. And bring more people with you," I told him. And he did.

By the fourth time at Sueby's, there were around a hundred and twenty people there. The place was absolutely packed. We new we could play at bigger clubs, but how? That's where Cecil came in. Since Sueby's had a stage, Cecil, and Linda Sueby, the owners, let us practice on their stage Sunday afternoons.

Tin and Rock each had bought twin amps. Crate one-hundred-fifty -watt heads with some good effects and two twelve-inch speaker cabinets. Probably top effects for the time.

I was still playing my Warwick axe through the Peavey two-hundred-watt head and a four by fifteen cabinet. We had each plugged our own mics into our own amps but that doesn't sound too good. But Sueby's had a sound system for the microphones.

"We need a good power amp for our vocals," Rock told us. Tin and I agreed so we went to our local music store, *A Plethora of Music*, and did the rent to own thing. We got a twelve channel, two-hundred-watt power amp and two loud-speakers and two monitor speakers. *We'll have it payed off in a year or so, right, guys*, I'm thinking? Now we could run all our sound through this set up and be loud enough for any stage, or so we thought.

Our first fun gig really showed us that we needed more power. We played at Tin's brother's block party one weekend. Our first outdoor gig. That was a blast 'cause it was like family. Well for Tin and Rock it was, but I was still just the bass player. It was a fun time, but it just wasn't loud enough.

We went on late after finally getting the extra amp and speakers, but once we, and the crowd, could here properly, we rocked. We could here ourselves just fine, and the partiers a few doors down could finally here us.

Now back at Sueby's we could play without their equipment, but we used them anyway. I met a lot of old friends there in my old stomping grounds and met a lot of new ones including Jennifer. She was a blonde-haired beauty.

We played at Sueby's almost every Saturday night for the whole winter and into the spring. Jennifer was there every show and came with me to every practice she could. We were hooked on each other.

Tin was married to Virginia, (Ginny), and Rock was married to Lynn. I had just met my woman, Jennifer, and Bill had a longtime girl friend as well named Linda, and all four women became good friends. We often ate dinner out together, all eight of us.

One Sunday evening after practice at Sueby's, the girls told us to come back to Rock's for dinner. To our surprise, they had put some cash together and bought one of those new sixteen track cassette recorder, mixer machines.

Lynn started it off. "Honey, guy's, we understand how tuff it is to record all of these demos, so we all chipped in and got you guys a gift," as they giggled and clapped.

We spent hours, days, weeks, yes months working on record- ing our homegrown songs. Rock was the main writer, but we all, including Thriller, wrote songs too. Our demo tape for Sueby's now seemed like kid stuff with this new toy. We learned to record fairly good recordings.

Rock and his wife had now moved to Waukegan, not far from that waterfront *taste of* jam. That became our usual recording place. So now we spent most tuesday and thursday nights at Rocks, maybe every other saturday night and lot's of sunday days at Sueby's. I thought sure the girls would be really tired of it all by now, but they were having as much fun as we were. And they kept us fed.

Jennifer had become a good sound engineer. I guess I taught her well. Jennifer worked at a physical rehab place in Evanston, another six miles or so south of Sueby's where there are lots of bars and big clubs.

She took our demo tape and passed it around. By the middle

of May that year, we were invited to join a *Battle of the Bands* in Evanston.

There were eighty-seven bands that competed. The battle was a three daylong event. It started Friday evening at the Northeast College football stadium, Wilton Stadium.

The people who put this together really had it together. They set up the stage around the twenty-yard line and the crowd watched from the stands and rows of chairs on the field. From my viewpoint on stage, it looked like fifteen or twenty rows on the field.

Thursday, we all agreed by phone calls that we would meet for an early dinner tomorrow in Evanston, 'cause we were told over the phone, that we'd be on around seven thirty or eight.

We drove down to Wilton Stadium. Our quickest route was down 41. Twenty minutes down to Skokie Rd., right, then left curve over the bridge and then left onto Lake Street. Then east, I don't know, eight or ten minutes. Then a couple of other short turns and there we were.

I don't think that I could lead you this day to that door we were arrowed to, but I do remember it like it was last week. It was one of those soda-pop kind of lines, you know, it takes a whole can of coke to go through. Then we had to go to another line with our gear, but at least we were going in.

Rock had this idea to use a lawnmower base and wheels and move the big gear. I was all for it and Tin said he wanted to try and improve his small cart. His was with a golf bag rig. I'm not a golfer, but I could see how it could work for other equipment to.

I'd seen an upright bass player one time that had made a cart for his bass from a rolling golf bag and his worked great. I found one at a garage sale and both mine and Tin's worked really well.

We had unpacked our loud jammin' axes and amps and all the gear out of the cars, but we still had to carry them from the gravel parking lot into the stadium. I'm glad we had those rolling carts cause that stuff is heavy. Once we got around towards the door and

had lost the gravel, we all looked at each other. *Awesome* we all agreed with a look, all wondering what was going to be next.

Once we got in, we went down a long hall. Some of us went to our left. Other bands went to the right. We went into a big bar, restaurant room that had all the tables and chairs removed. There were a bunch of other holding areas of different sizes.

While we were waiting for our spot in the light, I took a walk and went by a door with a sign that read *BAND OUTDOOR WAITING AREA*. I looked out and saw that I was way back-stage at about the 50-yard line. I went straight back to Tin and said, "Let's go have a smoke, and grab Rock."

The third band was playing when we got outside and there was about fifty wanna be rock heroes out there, and yes, us too. They had set up speakers for us 'cause the back-stage sound is really dull and flat back that far. We went back in and told everyone. We had to take turns so that no one would steal our stuff. The girls would usually go outside together, but not every time.

"Hey, man, what's your band, I'm in a band called Sweetwater," some guy says.

"Hey, how's it going with you? We're "Chicane," Tin and I said just about together. We met *The Cosmic Stargazers,* and *The Blick Blickman Blues Band.* We met a guy from a band called *Measuring Tape.* He was cool and we hung out for a while. There was a wide variety of bands, just like the wide variety of people in the army. We beat most of those bands that night but not *Measuring Tape.* The bald guy from the band was cool, but I can't remember his name.

We went on stage around ten pm or so, twenty-third in line, and a lot later than the phone person had told us. We played our three songs, and in my view, pretty darn good. We hooked it good during the first song, *Route Seventeen*, one of our homegrown songs. I remember messing up a little during Neil's *Southern Man*, and the third song, *Dust My Broom*, was the killer tune. We hooked the blues sound perfectly. We just *WOWed* the crowd.

When we were hauling our stuff back down the long hallway, I thought *out to the gravel pull area again*. After we secured our stuff in our vehicles, we went back in for a few more brats and meet other music people and hang out back-stage for a while.

That's when a guy from the contest came up to me and Rock. He asked me "Who's the boss of you guys?"

Rock and I kind of looked at each other and said simultaneously, "Where's Tin," We called Tin over from a few feet away for the three-way call. Thriller and his lady had already left for the night.

This guy, Francis Scoper, told us to make sure we are here tomorrow morning, like bright and early. "Just be here, OK," he said to us. Then he just left.

I would guess he went to tell some of the other bands that they might make it, also, maybe. Then we said goodbye to some new friends and took off for home.

It took twice as long to get home than going there 'cause we went all the way up to Waukegan. After dropping everything into Rock's garage and a quick listen to the tape they gave us, we headed for home. Jennifer and I didn't get home till well after one am. Wow, what a fun night.

Saturday morning, we got up early. After driving back to Waukegan to haul gear, and south again we all met back at the stadium and gathered inside. We got there by eight. The same drag across the same gravel parking lot and into the same holding room. I was so glad they served breakfast, lunch and dinner there. Everything was cooked on grills in the outside back-stage area. Man, I'm hungry.

Once we hunkered our stuff down, I went to get breakfast. I'm glad we got there early, cause the line was already long, ten people. While Jennifer and I were enjoying our breakfast, Linda and Tin showed up. By the time Rock and Lynn got there, Jennifer and I had finished our food and Linda and Tin were just starting there's. No biggie. Rock and Lynn were right behind. We all ate and hung out a while we were waiting.

Francis Scoper had just told me we wouldn't be on for probably four more hours. We'll see.

So here I am on a hot muggy sunny July afternoon. *I guess we're still in*, and *I know we're still here just so they'll tell us to go home*, were both in my thoughts. Tin had that look too. That's Tin and me. Rock on the other hand figured that if the judges take a long time, then that's good. Jennifer agreed, trying to chill me out. I was quite nervous for some reason.

"This is a really big production," I kept telling Jennifer. She would just give me that *no kidding, genius*, look.

There were all kinds of bands there, from country to punk. From head banging, to folk rock, every kind of band, even some totally weird stuff. Tin said it was the wildest time he had ever had, "Are you kidding," Rock said, "I've never seen anything like this."

"Your right," I said, "This is wild, but let's not forget why we're here."

Around one or so Saturday afternoon, Francis grabs Bill and tells him "You guys are on in twenty minutes."

"We are on in nineteen minutes," Bill yells excitedly while running up to us.

"All right, let's go," I barked, like a drill sergeant. *Yea, yea, bla-bla-bla*, was the only response I heard, but everyone was moving.

We got back-stage within five or six minutes and there was one band still ahead of us. Guess what? It's our new friends Measuring Tape. "Hey Darien," I hollered up the stairs, "break a leg."

"Yes, that's my name." He yelled back down, "Same to you. Buddy." I won't talk much about them and they're sound, but they were very different.

All right, we're up next. Killer wasn't to thrilled cause he had to play the house drums, but at least, he had told me, he could rearrange them some. I was set up to Bill's left and Tin's rig was forward and to my left. Rock was on our right. The monitors they had there were awesome. I really thought that if I couldn't see Rock, I couldn't here him. Boy, was I wrong. The sound was awesome.

Now it's getting down to crunch time. I know by experience that if I can hear myself well, I can play well. If I can hear myself great, I can rock. I could hear myself, and everyone else, perfectly.

We started playing *Diddley, Squiddely*, a song I wrote that the guys caught on to right away. It's a bouncy, choppy, almost blue grass kinda rockin' sound. If you've never heard of it, maybe you should buy some of our CD's. Just kidding. We did Neil's *Fourteen Junkies* and our own, *Me and Edgar*. The lead ending Tin did on Edgar made me think we had hit the jackpot. It was sweet.

We pulled our stuff off the stage after we were done and as we were heading down that long hall again, I said to Jennifer, "I hope this is just the beginning."

She told me, "It is sweetie."

"Good," I said, "let's go eat." We hung out awhile and listened to more bands. We saw Francis Scoper before we got to the exit out to the gravel pull area.

He said to us all, "You guys just might take this thing. The judges are thrilled with you guys, so be here early tomorrow and look sharp. See you."

Once again, back to Rock's to drop everything off, and *see you in eight hours*. Only tonight it was only eleven thirty when Jennifer and I got home.

Sunday, ten am, we were there, starting day three. It was down to twelve bands, and we were still in it. We had seven songs that we had practiced, and we needed to start the list all over.

While we were waiting, I saw the guy from *Measuring Tape*, and he seemed very nervous. "This is really nerve racking," I said.

He responded with "no kidding, I think I've lost half of my hair today." That was a joke 'cause he was bald anyway. I saw another guy I had met the day before who also looked nervous. He told me his marriage might be at stake. *Good luck with all of that*, my thoughts.

I had an Italian Beef sandwich for lunch, and Jennifer had a chicken sandwich. We shared the fries. We would have shared a drink, but she drinks the diet style, while I like the classic style cola.

By Sunday afternoon it was down to six bands, and we were still there. We had to play one more set of three songs.

On our last song, *Rollin*, and as it turned out, sixteen measures before the end of the song, *twawawawawang*. I really believe that if Tin hadn't broken that D string we just might have won, but third isn't too bad, though. Rock is holding our third-place trophy this year, but I get it next year, and around it goes.

Wilmington's

Let me tell you a little bit a bought Wilmington's cool basement. During the time while I was playing at Sueby's, and before, and going through the *Battle* days with *Chicane*, as we were calling ourselves, I was still spending some time at Wilmington's, once every other week or so.

I met this guy who took over an old job I had had. He was the next new mechanic at the old rental yard and Rob, the manager and I were still friends and Rob introduced us. We hit it off right then and there.

This knucklehead, and I say that in good jest, Greg Gussell, went by Gus, was the rockinest, coolest, lead kinda guy I had ever jammed with, and I said EVER jammed with. We really got a groove goin'. He told me a couple of months later that he didn't know what to make of me at first.

Rob only told him I was a bass player before that first meeting. I was wearing a cowboy hat, cowboy boots, and big cowboy belt buckle and headphones. He was wondering, he told me, *what is this guy listening to?*

I had a portable cassette player with my headphones. I had only been back from Texas for a year or so and still had some of the old habits, you know, the bass player from Texas. When I gave him the headphones, he listened for a moment or two and then pulled them off and asked, "How can a dude dressed like you, the boots and all, could possibly be listening to the chili peppers?" We've been friends since then, him and his lovely wife Cindy.

Gus liked to call her, mostly for us guys, and she went along with it, *Sault City Cindy*. She was from Sault City, and I had heard of it from the ski shop I was working at at the time, ski and patio, that is. There was a cool ski hill about three hours or so from here that was called Kelmont Mountain. It was just outside Sault City. I've skied there a bunch of times.

Now, Gus was just too cool. He had a boat, a different boat every couple of years. I went out on his boats as often as I could, but it was only about fifteen times or so.

One time we brought our acoustic guitars with us, and my bass was a big, wide, deep, *Kramer* four-stringer. It was probably around eight or eight-thirty, pm, just about dark, and I thought we had the anchor down. We were engine off, just sitting. The lake wasn't very big and there were no other boats hanging out near us, so, "let's play a while," Gus says.

The water was still, but there was a small undertow that I realized almost too late, that was slowly moving us towards the shore. Now, we were busy jammin' and were somewhat oblivious about our where abouts when I saw the boat slips getting very close. We were hardly moving.

As we got closer, I quickly put my bass down and climbed onto the side of the boat and put my foot up to stop us from smashing into the peer. I slowed the boat just enough to keep from spilling our beers. We probably would have hit only hard enough to make us kind of lose our balance, but it could have damaged the boat.

Gus was very apologetic and thanked me for stopping the boat and I said "Why didn't you finish your lead." We all laughed, and thanks for good times.

The next time I was out on Gus' boat we were on Lake Michigan.

It was pretty choppy and the waves were spraying onto the boat. What I didn't realize was that my bass got wet from some of those sprays. A few days later, while I was at Wilmington's, my roommate told me he heard a sound like an acoustic guitar had fallen over. It turned out that it hadn't fallen over, but the bridge broke loose from the body and that's what went *twang*.

I still have that bass and maybe someday I'll revive it. I have fixed other guitars, and I'm getting a good handle on it. As I investigated that guitar mishap, I noticed I had put steel, rather than bronze strings on it. Steel strings are for solid body electric guitars not acoustics. Oh well, live and learn.

I brought Gus down to Wilmington's one evening after Gus had jammed a few times with Rock, Tin and myself. He was hooked on the spot. "Wilmington," he said, "This is so cool, and can I come back and jam again?"

Wilmington had a boat also, so they got along right away, and we did Thursday's down at Willmington's as often as we could. We thought we had a pretty good power trio going. A power trio, for you light weights, is one guitarist, one bassist, and one drummer.

That was when it was just the three of us without all those fly-by-night guys who would show up once every couple of months or so. Hey, ask your guitar player friends this question. *What do you call a guy who hangs out with musicians?* The answer is, *A Drummer*. Anyway, I digress.

Then Wilmington said he had a new employee coming from Wyoming, and he was a keyboard player. We were psyched. I had never jammed with a keyboardist more than once before.

I remember some nights down at Wilmingtons when he would run upstairs to see what Christina, his wife, needed. While he was gone, Gus and I would trade licks. He would play something with his back turned, and I would try and figure out the key. Once I did, he would change to something different and when I would figure that one out, he would change again, and when I figured out that one, on to another one, around it goes. That was a good education.

But now, we all agreed, *we have us a key player.* Then it turned out, Witt was a keyboard player, but he was really a guitar player, and man, he could play.

After five or six months with the four of us, Gus asks, "why don't we play out, like at The Rainbow Club?" They understood the seriousness of *Chicane*, but I was still interested in playing out. This, after all, started before the *battle* days. This was really along the same days as Sueby's early years.

Wilmington's was so cool, like I said, for the different guitarists, but also the togetherness with the four of us, the camaraderie of the place. It was almost always seven fifteen pm or so (once everybody was plugged in and loud), that we'd play till eight fifteen or so. One song after another, and another, good jammin'. "I need a rest," someone would say. We would all agree with a nod and *Yea!*"

We'd go outside and some of us would have a smoke, and some would not. We'd talk about this singer or that guitarist or that band or whatever. We just wanted a pause.

Sometimes Wilmington would bum a smoke cause his wife didn't want him smoking. "I just have to have a smoke from time to time, you know," Wilmington would plead.

"Sure, Wilmington, just don't tell your wife, buddy." We'd play for another forty-five minutes or so and that would be it.

"See you girls next week," Wilmington would usually say. Next week was always the same; you could set your watch by it. Same drum time, same drum channel.

It didn't matter who was there jammin', we all had fun. Early on down there I do remember a top-notch keyboard player who stopped by one night. It was Chris Eilbourne, who brought down a full eighty-eight key instrument. I mean full sized. It took four of us two separate trips down the stairs. It also had an amp and two speakers. *Four people, two trips, not bad.* and *that is one cool key board,* was what I was thinking. He even played the *Peanuts theme* song. I mean this guy should've been a pro. I was flabbergasted. Instead, he was just an average tradesman kind of guy. Wilmington tried for years to get him to come back down there, but never while I was there. Gus, on the other hand, really rocked things up.

Wilmington and I had been playing with his high school buddy Mike, the boss at the ski and patio store. Rock and Tin even played down there with us a couple of times, but not with Mike anyway. So, it was a real thrill to have Gus down there. He was the first, and I think still the best, real cool lead rocker I had ever jammed with, even better than Bullard, except that I hadn't heard Bullard's playing since the army.

Witt, George Wittman, was a specialist in Wilmington's business and a fantastic guitar player. He was a good keyboard player also. He was different than Gus, but probably just as good. *This is so cool* I thought, *two good guitarists, this couldn't be better* thoughts *were* in my head.

We got a gig at The Rainbow Club as Gus had suggested. This whole band was different from Chicane 'cause it was, as we all knew, just for fun, and, temporary. We still put a lot of work into it. I was there every practice night.

I met a guy in the Rainbow Club shortly before he started working there. I'll never forget Jimmie Jackson, who was known as Jack, 'cause of his *jack of all trade's* knowledge of music and computers.

He was also a wizard behind the bar. He really didn't play, but he understood the technical theory. He played keyboards good enough to record midi stuff though. He actually had received a minor college degree in sound recording, and he had been around a lot of bands.

I wanted to hang out with him, 'cause if you were into music of any sort, he would push you to continue. He ended up running the Rainbow Club for ten or twelve months.

I asked him if there was room in the Saturday night band schedule for a local band. "You know we're friends, but if the boss is going to give the OK, I'll need a demo tape," he said. Here we go again with the demo tape stuff.

Down at Wilmington's, we only had that cassette recorder, but guess what, we still had the cheap mics. We practiced three songs once a week for four or five weeks and then recorded them. *alright, we got us a demo, let's go,* were our confirmed thoughts. Jack sent it to Rainbow, the owner, who I also knew, and he said, "hire 'um."

We called ourselves D'Arranged, what a cool name, huh? I'll tell you about that later....

Jack was important part of my musical education. He had a way of making you think a little different, make you look at your craft in a whole new light. It happened down in Romer's basement.

Romer was a guy that also hung out with us at the Rainbow Club. This club wasn't like the clubs back in Texas; this was just a name, just another bar, just like in Waco. On I go again.

Romer had a cool house. Not his, but he lived there. He had the best home sound system I had ever heard. The only problem for me was, where do I plug in?

Romer wasn't a guitar player, but a guitar lover, a music lover. He couldn't play any instruments, but he loved music and wanted to learn how it all worked.

A lot of the things Jack taught us those nights don't really show up in music books, but the explanations Jack told Romer really had an impact on me. Things about the same timing from different measures, or how to count beats a different way, you know, different stuff. Funky kinda stuff.

Romer was an electrician who thought he was a genius with electricity. My Army training told me, maybe not. Romer had some scary hook ups, but I figured, as long as we didn't overload his system, we were okay.

We would hang down there and play song after song and try to record them on Romer's cassette recorder.

He wanted to know how the different sounds needed to be

recorded differently. I tried to explain to him that it wasn't the instruments, but the guy recording, and his recorder that made the difference.

He had a huge mixing board. I don't think to this day that he understood how to use it. Jack and I could only explain so much to a guy who just didn't get it. Oh well, we tried.

I thought this time at the Rainbow Club would be fun. As I guessed, it was. The big problem was I didn't realize it at the time, but I had a problem with my bass. The jack where I plug the cord into was shorting out and my sound was cutting in and out. Mostly out. I'm glad we didn't record it 'cause I would have tossed it out.

Three months later we played there again and this time I rocked as well as the rest of us. Tin and Rock were there with a video camera going and singing along with us.

We did all cover songs as I probably told you. The second time was even better than the first time.

About six months later we played there again. This time we really hit it right. Tin and Rock were there to watch and afterwards, Tin told me, "Dude, you really rock." I thought that was so cool since he was a rockin' buddy.

Sometimes on Saturday nights, if I wasn't busy with Rock and Tin, I would go over to Wilmington's. He would get two or three or four other musicians to come by and jam, as I've told you.

Once there was a pedal steel guitar player who just happened to be traveling from L. A. to New York, who knew a guitar player who Wilmington knew, who showed up with his pedal steel guitar buddy. I don't remember either of their names, but that made for an interesting jam.

Another time it was Gus and a friend of Wilmington's named Bob Nelis. Bob was a good guitar player and a keyboardist. Bob was there many times, actually.

One time a guitarist named Clyde Davis was there with his friend, Joe Spack. I wasn't supposed to be there that night, but Rock was sick, and our regular jam was cancelled so I showed up. Clyde was playing a four string hollow body bass while Joe brought along a twelve-string bass. Clyde was a guitar player who also owned a couple of cool basses. The twelve-string bass was set up just like a twelve-string guitar, but instead of two strings for each string on a regular guitar, it had three strings for each of the normal four strings for a bass. What a great sound it had. The four-string hollow body sounded great, but the twelve-stringer sounded awesome. I got to play both basses a few times throughout the evening.

This is so cool, I was thinking. I could right a book about all the guys I played with down at Wilmington's, but that's another story all together.

I spent about a dozen years or so hanging out down at Wilmington's, but I haven't talked to him for a couple of years now. I'm just to busy these days. Sorry, I don't mean to get ahead of my self though.

Onward I Go

After we almost won the battle of the bands, life was just about to change. I never liked the idea of a *battle* when it came to rock 'n' roll cause in my mind it's all about the music, not competition. But it did get some local clubs around the Chicago area to want us to play. Tin and I gave our numbers as contacts and the calls were overwhelming. Jennifer was basically my secretary, and she couldn't believe the amount of calls we got. Most of them were small little dives all around Chicago and the suburbs.

The first place we played was Sueby's, our old stomping grounds, of course. We couldn't let Nello down. The place that Saturday night was more than packed. There were thirty or forty people outside that weren't let in 'cause it was so packed. I've never played a bar *that* packed. The bar was probably well over the legal limit of people inside. Nello opened the doors to let the sound out into the parking lot till the cops said it was to loud for the neighbors. It was a cool night, though. I had to tell Nello that we had many other offers, and we could only play there every other month or so.

The next gig we accepted I wish we hadn't. It was a bar in Chicago on Rush Street, Martin's Mark-Up. Kind of a sleazy look-ing place, but the pay sounded good. It all started okay. Nine-thirty start, three forty-five-minute sets. It all seemed normal. Then half-way through the third set, just after midnight, a fight broke out between some of the patrons. It got pretty bad when the two main bad guys fought each other right up to the stage. Then they came onto the stage, crashing into Rock. Just as he was getting into a bar chord lead kind of thing, *CRASH*, one guy hits the other right into Rock knocking him into his amp and onto the floor. We tried to keep playing but to no avail.

The security guys ran up right away and pulled these two idiots away, but it was to late. Rocks guitar was broken. We apologized to the rest of the crowd and said we may be back. The crowd cheered us, but we decided later that that was it for that place. I was getting good at fixing guitars, so I fixed that one, but enough is enough.

Rock used to have a big dog, a Newfoundland, you know, a hundred and twenty pounds or so, and one time when Rock set his guitar down on it's stand and walked away, Colby followed. One of his back feet hooked the cable and the guitar fell over. *Whack*, it hit the floor. Well, it hit the floor hard and broke the neck. "Don't worry guys, I can fix it," I told them, and I did. A couple of months later, Tin's dog knocked over another guitar and it broke the same way. I fixed that one too. I think I have glued seven or eight or so guitars of ours and other peoples back together. I've become a pretty good guitar tech over the years. Any time one of us bought a new guitar, I checked it out to make sure it was set up properly.

The next place we went to play at least seemed much better than the last one. Palatine is a suburb north-west of Chicago that has lots of bars that host local bands. Wilfords had a stage that could probably hold a full orchestra. I think it was bigger than the stage I played on back in the army at that old movie theater that had those cool little sound-proof rooms. The rest of the bar was huge. It could hold around two hundred people or so.

We got on stage to start our show around nine that night but not after a scary event earlier that evening. We set up about seven and did the usual sound check, then packed up our axes and went for dinner. Jennifer and I got back before the others and found the cops there. As it turned out, two guys had tried to steel some of our stuff including my amp head. These guys almost walked out of the door with a bunch of our stuff. It turned out that the staff was so busy with the crowd that came to see us that they didn't notice these two perpetrators. An old friend, Jim Chaplinsky, whom I hadn't seen in a few years, had heard I was playing there and came to see me play. He was hanging out near the back door and asked this guy who had my amp head in his hand why he was leaving with it. "Are you the bass player?" he asked.

"Yes, but I'm going to use my other one," he told J.C., as I knew him. J.C. didn't buy it and called the waitress over while keeping this guy inside. They already had cleared out our mics and Tin's amp. The other guy was still inside and hid amongst the crowd.

The waitress quickly went to the manager and told him, and he called the cops. If it hadn't been for J.C., who knows how much stuff they would have gotten from us.

The show turned out really well with the crowd yelling and cheering us on all night. I made sure J.C. drank for free all night long. It was really good to see him again. He became our best groupie and our security dude. He was with us from then on, even hanging around at the practice nights. Wilfords even hired a security guy for all their band nights from then on. We came back and played there many times after that. You just never know in this rock and roll business.

That's when I got a call from Francis Scoper, the guy from the battle thing. "Hi, this is Francis Scoper, do you remember me?" he asked.

"Yes Francis, how's it going?" I replied.

"Good, I'm currently working for Claude Bellows who runs the Regal Room, have you heard of it?" he asked. The Regal Room was the biggest nightclub outside of Chicago at the time.

"Yes of course, who hasn't," I told him.

"Well, I told my boss about you guys and the battle deal and how I thought you guys should have won it. I also told him about the clubs that you've been playing at." He responded.

"How do you know where we've been playing?" I asked. He told me it's his job to watch good bands and we were one band he was interested in.

"I was at Sueby's, Martin's and Wilfords and you guys keep getting better, and I want you to play The Regal."

"Really?" was the only response I could muster.

"Listen, I can get you Saturday nights for as long as you hold a crowd if you're interested," he proclaimed.

"What's the pay?" I asked. He said we should talk it over and call him back. "Sure, come by on Sunday at our practice night and we'll all talk," I said, all excited. I gave him the address and time and he told me he would be there.

I immediately called Tin and set up a conference call with Rock and Bill and told them about my conversation with Scoper. We were all thrilled and couldn't wait till that meeting. I was ecstatic.

We were supposed to meet at seven that evening. We were there, but where's Scoper? Now it's eight and no sign of him. "He's not coming," Killer said four or five times.

"Maybe something came up," I said.

"Relax, he'll be here soon," I begged. Then we all jumped, *ding-dong*, went the doorbell. We all jumped up and went for the door.

J.C. was the one to answer, since he was our security guy, and asked "Francis?"

"Yes, sorry I'm late but there was an accident on the highway, so it took me a while to get here. So, let's get down to business," he explained.

"First let's relax and have a drink, what would you like, Francis." I said as I escorted him in.

He said, "call me Scoper, and a beer would sound good." We sat down and yakked for a while and relaxed, as I suggested. You know, the guys were way too anxious. He explained that every band he suggested needed to be vetted by the bosses.

I asked all the guys, "Do you think we have what it takes?"

They all responded, "YES."

"Okay, where do we go from here, fame or failure?" I asked. *Regal, Regal, Regal* was the chant. "OK, what's the deal with the Regal," I asked? Scoper told us it would be fifteen a night.

"Fifteen Hundred a night, no way?" was Tin's response. I was just as stunned.

Rock walked away in disbelief, but walked back and said, "Are you sure?" I even asked if he had lost his mind. Frank said he was authorized to hire us for five Saturday nights in a row at fifteen hundred a show. *WOW,* we sat back and exclaimed amongst ourselves with high fives. How could we not take it?

"Let's do it," I said vibrantly. We all agreed simultaneously, with a big, loud, *Let's Do It.* This would be our biggest payday yet. The battle gig only paid seven hundred and fifty. Now we had to get our stuff together, an entire night's show and new material. That means three or four forty-five-minute sets. "Guys, we've got our work cut out for us," I vociferated.

The next day I called Rock and asked what he thought about lots of more nights of practice. He bounced right up and said, "If we're gonna play this place, we gotta get a move on." That conversation started a Monday, Wednesday, Friday, and Saturday, all out jam session. And I played an hour or two each of the other nights just playing under my headphones.

Some of those nights were awesome jams, but I won't kid you, we got kind of huffy from time to time. We were learning a new song one time when I thought I had the timing right, when Killer said I was wrong. We played that part of the song at least ten or twelve times. Eventually Killer agreed with me, and he found the beat. Tin and I had some griefs too, as well as Rock and Tin, but we all worked through it. By the time The Regal gig date started, we were ready. We had learned to learn as well as jam. Things looked good.

The Regal Room wasn't just a room, but a concert hall. All of us, girls included, stopped by the Friday afternoon before our first show. We couldn't believe the size of this place. That big bar I played at back in Texas was bigger, but this place wasn't a bar (or three). It had rows and rows of seating. This place could easily seat two or three thousand, with the balconies. Jennifer and I walked all around the whole place to look at the view of the stage. Jennifer said, "I don't think there's a bad seat in the place."

"I know what you mean," I said, "They all look good."

Killer Bill was getting more hyper every minute. "This is going to be great," he kept yelling, "I'll be drumin' to the world." We all figured our positions on the stage.

"I've got like three hundred square feet just for me," Tin exclaimed.

"Yeah, me too," hailed Rock. Now I could stand along side Tin and Rock instead of back, along side of Killer's drums. How cool is that. It was an anxious ride home that night.

We got there about three that Saturday afternoon and set our stuff up. There were six people there to help us in any way we needed. Again, I was thinking that now we've hit it big, since we didn't have to hook up any thing except to plug in our guitars. And the sound system was awesome. We each had two monitors pointing up at us. Behind stage, well actually off stage left, were three tall racks of sound equipment, and speakers everywhere around the seats.

Four o'clock or so we were set and the lead sound guy, Neil Zumwalt, said it was time for our sound check. "Cool, guys, this is what it's all about," I told everyone. Jennifer gave me a big kiss and went into the seats, around row twenty. Ginny and Lynn joined her. Killer's girlfriend, Linda stayed back by the drums with her man.

We played my song, Rollin', and we hit it almost perfect. Zumwalt said over his mic that it sounded good but he needed one more. I figured at least one more, maybe three total. I was right. After the second song, Gimme Money, one of my songs again, I knew we needed one more. The vocals weren't right to my ear. "Hey Neil," I asked, "Can we get more monitors?"

"Yes, give me another song," he said. After the third song, *Used to It*, one of Tin's, we all agreed the sound was there.

"Man, that sounds cool," Tin called out over his mic.

"All right," Zumwalt told us, "Chow time you guys, I'll see you all back here at nine." And off we went, with our guitars. We always kept our guitars with us while on the road.

I don't remember what the other guys did, but Jennifer and I had a big pasta meal, like Neil Young would do the night before a big show. We went to an Italian place Jennifer's work friends had told her about. I had Fettuccine and nothing else besides a drink, beer of course. Just pasta and sauce. It was delicious. Some of her friends from work were there and later came to see the show. The couple we sat by were sound engineers for a near by testing lab company. They knew all about EMI, or electro magnetic interference, and Quentin, Quentin Skaggs told me his hobby was audio recording. Over the next few weeks, between jams and preparing for more gigs, I went to talk more inclusively with Quentin about recording, which I was completely interested in, and he and I set up time to work on that situation. I can't believe the knowledge I learned from Quentin. He taught me more about the sound thing than Jimmy Jack had. *I'm learning from the best,* I thought. But anyway, I digress.

Eight thirtyish we got back and milled around a bit in the lobby. Quentin and his wife Sandra came and talked for a minute or so when Sandra said, "we better go get our seats, shouldn't you be on stage?"

I looked at my watch. "You're right, come on Jen, let's go. Talk to you guys after the show."

"See ya," Quentin says over his shoulder. We worked our way

over to the side row heading towards stage right and up the four or five stairs and back behind the rows of curtains.

Jennifer gave me a kiss and said, "Good luck sweetie, I'll be watching with the girls." She's always such a romantic.

When I got all the way back stage, Killer wasn't there. "You guys tuned?" I asked.

"You betcha, is Killer with you?" Tin piped up.

"No, I haven't seen him since sound check, but I'll be tuned shortly," I chuckled as I said. Tin was always nervous right before a show.

Tin barked back, "Yea, but we've only got fifteen minutes till show time."

"He'll be here, relax," I tried to reassure him.

After I tuned, I went over to Rock 'cause he had a funny grin in his look at me. "I know that look," I prodded, "what are you up to now?"

He leaned in as to whisper and said, "Bill's been here for half an hour but Tin thinks he bailed on us."

"Why would he think that," I asked with my eyebrows very raised?

"Oh, I don't know, someone might have suggested it to him," he said with a question in his voice.

"Okay, how long do I have to go along with this?" I asked Rock.

"Just a minute or two, here comes Tin, hold your self." We were both laughing pretty good at that time.

"Where is Bill," Tin questioned loudly.

"Right here buddy, what's up," Killer said like out of nowhere, "where else would I be."

"Rock, I'm gonna kill you," Tin kind of yelled as he went for Rock. Killer stepped in to break it up and all of us were cracking up. "Alright troops," Tin all of a sudden barked, "Let's go rock," and off we went. That first set was the best time I have ever felt playing my bass.

I was so comfortable that first set that it spooked me. *No, no,* my thoughts started thinking. *Pay attention.* And then I was back, rockin'. Not like when I was younger, less experienced, but still that feeling that you just cannot get up onto that stage, but when you finally start playing, it's just so good. During the middle part of the second set, Rock was jamming his lead thing on Memphis Heartbroken, when he broke his D string, but he limped through it as best he could till the end of the song. He still kept on rockin' even when wounded. What a trooper, huh?

After that song, thanks to the staff techies, his other guitar was handed to him before the next song. Before the show, this rodie asked us if he could tune our guitars for us. "Not me, thanks, I'll be tuning my own, but thanks for asking," I said. After all a bass usually stays in tune all night.

Tin told him "Yes, but if it's out, I'll be really, really upset." Then Tin told him he was kidding and said, "Yes my friend, tune away, thank you, sir." By the time that string broke, poor ol' Daryl Wyenn was scrambling to grab Tins other guitar and get it to him just in time for the next song. How cool is that. Our second time at the Regal, we had a very strange thing happen.

You know we like Neil Young, but we found out there was a group of people who had seen us play and were Neil fans. They had grouped together and were there. Every time we would start a Neil song, this group of fans would haunt and holler, they would yell and scream. It was almost scary. They came back-stage afterwards to meet us. *We have fans,* I was thinking. *Next come groupies, yuck.*

During the Monday etc. type nights, things were tough. We were trying to learn two or three songs every week. That's a tough schedule for any band at our low level; after all, we were just the four of us. Learning a new song is tough for four guys to put together, but the reward is awesome when you play it on stage. I think the fans at the Regal really did like us.

Our third night at the Regal was very uneventful. Our first and second set went by so quick, you know, no one screaming or dancing wildly, but no one was bored. They were dancing and generally just having a good time. On our last song, and it always seems to come down to the last song, halfway through, Killer puts his foot right through the kick drum. I don't mean his foot broke the drumhead, I mean it broke and his pedal and his foot went into the kick drum. We finished the song OK with the crowd applauding Killer for hanging on, but we were all bummed it happened that way.

The fourth and fifth time we played at the Regal, everything seemed perfect. The crowd loved us, and we played just fine.

After the last show while we were loading our stuff into the vans for the long ride home, a guy came up to us in the parking lot, and said "Hi, I'm Ritchie Novack. I'm with Dreadfull Records, and we are interested in getting you guys into the studio for a couple of sessions. What do you guys think?"

I asked, "How'd you get in here?"

We all laughed and then Tin asked, "what do you mean a couple of sessions, Mr. Novak?"

He responded with "My name is Ritchie and I am offering you guys some professional recording time to maybe put an album together." I sat down on Rocks amp and Tin and Rock leaned against one of the vans. Killer was pacing like crazy. Our home recording stuff was OK, but a pro shop? After a moment or so, I pulled the guys together and had a brief. Afterwards I got Ritchie's number and told him we'll be in touch. Before we all drove off, we agreed that studio time, and album thoughts were really cool.

6

Studio Time

There were many other clubs we played at for a few weeks till we really decided to get serious with the studio stuff. During those weeks we spent our time between new songs and our old songs, a couple of nights at clubs, and some weeks one night a week learning the new, big studio. Most nights a week I would be playing somewhere. The thought was that we shouldn't have to work this hard, after all we all had day jobs. *So, let's go studio full time*, we all decided, at night anyway.

We had our own little studio equipment, but not the good stuff the pros have, and we kind of had it right in the way we recorded, but this sounded really cool.

I called Ritchie and we agreed to start sessions three times a week till the album was done. The next Sunday we were there. One O'clock sounded like a good time to me. Now we all knew the drill, but our first time to the studio was so different.

That first time we met Mark Clark, the head tech guy, and he took care of us. We had driven to Kenosha, about an hour drive from my place, and had parked in a four dollar an hour lot. We asked Mark about parking and our equipment situation, and he immediately sent us back to our cars, had us drive to the underground parking in the building and up the freight elevator with the staff hauling everything for us.

We went to the second floor then down a long, long hallway. We turned right and went about ten feet to a door on our right. When we went in, I could understand why the long hall. This huge room reminded me of the old movie theater building back in Texas. This room though was only one story tall, unlike movie theaters tall ceilings. Inside this room were small chambers like in Texas, but they were a little bigger and strategically placed. One large room was against the far long wall and to our left. There were moveable walls that were thick and padded and amps and mics were everywhere.

Tin reminded me of a small studio we checked out once a few years before that was made from an old grocery store. "This place is so much cooler then Eakes studio, remember that place."

"Yah," I responded, "I thought that place was awesome, this place puts that place to shame big time."

We chuckled a little when killer pokes in and says, "where are the drums, they said they have better drums than mine and I can arrange things the way I want, where are they, I gotta find the drums."

"Chill Killer, see that room over there," as I pointed to the big room along the long wall, "head over there and take a look." He almost floated over.

Mark came in and showed us around a bit and said, "I see you figured out where the drum room is. You guys will play behind these walls to deaden the sound of your strings so the other guy's microphones won't pick it up. You will hear everything through your headphones, even me. Now will be the time to find a spot and set up your stuff, and by the way guys, let's have fun."

Then he walked away. Killer came back and said, "Wow, I get to play in my own soundproof room, do you think I'll hear OK through those headphones."

I said "hey, what'd you say?" Killer started to repeat himself and stopped.

"Nothing you haven't figured out already, except we play behind these walls," Rock tells him.

"How am I gonna groove with the bass if I can't see the bass," he asked in his hyper kind of way?

"Killer," I jumped in, "you don't have to see me to feel the groove. I'll hear you and you'll hear me just as if my amp was right next to you and I was jamming right there too." He didn't sound convinced, though, still bouncing a bit.

We all went about our tasks to set up our amps, guitars and adjust the mics. Killer changed all kinds of stuff with the drums. He even tried different thrones. I found my spot nearest to Killers room. I put the headphones on and immediately talked into the mic, "Is this thing on."

"Yes, it is, and what do you need," came a reply.

"Do these walls move, I mean I'd love to face the drum room if I could." "Yes, they slide in a circler motion from left to right. Move yours to the right," came the response. *Cool,* I thought as I was sliding the two ninety degreed walls in these little train track kind of grooves in the floor, *this should calm Killer down, now he'll be able to see me,* I thought. He noticed and gave me a big thumbs up.

After I plugged in and tuned, I put my bass down and went to see where Rock and Tin had set up. They too had found the headphones and had heard my conversation and had moved their walls so they could see each other. We couldn't be a front-to-front kind of thing, but we could all pretty much see each other's eyes if we needed to. After we were all tuned and Killer was set, we went into the room at the long end of the big room. That was, obviously enough to Tin and I, the control room.

Mark was in there with three other people, two guys and a cute woman. We all kind of looked at each other with that look of *don't even think about it.* Then those thoughts were gone when we all looked at the console, the board. It was huge. Mark explained it to us, "From the left to the right, the first eight controls are for you, Killer, and can I call you that?"

"Yea what-ever dude, I got eight mics on the drums?" he asked.

"Yes," Mark went on, "the next two are for Tin and his mic, the next two for Rock, and two for you," he said as he looked toward me.

"Alright guys, which song shall we do?" I asked. *Highway Forty-Seven*, seemed to be the conscientious thought, so we all agreed and off to our stations.

Recording order was drums first, then bass, and everything else afterwards so Killer thought he was on trial. "Why do I have to record first, I mean why me?" Killer sort of moaned to me quietly.

"Cool out dude," I whispered. He seemed to be OK through the first take. During the second take, he bobbled just a bit, and after the third take he went nutty. "I'm sorry, I think I just forgot how to play these things. What are these round things in front of me? I don't understand what they do," he seemed to almost yell.

"Chill, man, just play, we're all just playing," I told him through the mics and headphones. "Just pretend we're in your basement and I'm standing three feet away from your high hat, we'll jam just like that, OK?" After that he was just fine. Although it took us nine takes to get Killers drums down that Mark figured we could work with, that was it for that day's session.

"If we do this in the evening, an hour or two, we won't even get this much done," Mark reminded us, "That was only four hours, guys." We thanked him and said see you on Tuesday. We had all ridden up to Kenosha in Tin's minivan since we only needed room for our guitars, small amps and our gear bags, but I still road in the back with my feet on those bags. I slept most of the way home, dreaming of bigger stuff.

There we were, on stage at Madison Square Gardens, with the next stop, London. Seventh Street, downtown Manhattan, New York. We came in off I495 from Jersey. We went onto Dyer and then on to 34th street. We ended up on Broadway where we found a cool stop for dinner, early dinner, around four o'clock. Then we went on to 8th Ave. and into the Garden through some back door. It was a good thing we had an escort 'cause we never would have found it on our own.

The busses with our crew and the semi with our gear waited for us there. The crew unloaded and set up. When we got there, everything was set for a sound check. All we had to do was plug in and play, sort of like today's computers; you know, plug and play. The stage was set up around sections thirty-four through thirty-eight with everything behind us, sections one twenty-nine through one thirty-three and behind being backstage. The place was packed, I was guessing around ten or twelve thousand, but Rock said he thought it was probably more like twenty thousand. We jammed really well, and the crowd was going berserk. When we played *Cooler Than Cool*, a song I wrote, the whole place was on fire. The crowd yelled and screamed louder than our music was.

Then we did *Thirty Fourth Street Love Affair*, a Tin song, they were almost all singing along with us. After we finished our scheduled night of rock, the whole crowd, it seemed, were holding lighters up and calling us back for an encore. We came back on and did *DeWalt Tools Are the Best* and *Motorola Monkeys*, two new, kind of political anti-big business songs, and they cheered even louder.

When we finished our night and went backstage, there were news people there. *What do they want with us,* I wondered? We did a press conference thing and answered their questions, but I couldn't understand why us. Then it hit me; we finally made it in the big time. I couldn't have been happier, for all of us.

"Ding, Ding, Ding," I was hearing, and a light went on. Oh, I'm home, that was a good dream.

On Tuesday we headed back up to Kenosha to do it all over again. This time it was my turn with my bass. Things started much quicker since we now know where to park and where the elevator is and all of that. Since we weren't the only band they had up there, we had to rearrange things back to our way.

My little wall was turned away from the drums, so I had to turn it back and Rock and Tin likewise did their own turns. Once we were set up, I asked, "Is it bass time?"

"Get ready to rock my friend," came Mark's response. It only took me six takes playing along with Killer's drum recording and Rock and Tin playing live. Tin's guitar was next. He said he thought he could put his down in two or three takes. Wrong. It took him five tries, but it sounded great. Killer hung out in the sound booth while I played.

He told me he was getting hyper listening and watching me play to his drums without him playing. While Tin was playing, Killer and I joked how hard it was for us both to just sit and listen. Now when Rock's turn came up to play, Tin was in the booth with us and Mark had to tell us to quiet down, "I can't here ROCK, shhh…"

We finally finished Rocks takes. "Wow," Killer snapped, "It's ten thirty." That was it for the evening.

Thursday we were back and then finished with the vocals. We were all into the vocals together. Killer could now just sing instead of banging and singing. "Cool," Tin said, "One song down, nine to go."

Mark asked, "see you guy's Saturday, early?" We all agreed. On the way home we talked about the album we were trying to put together and figured it would take one hundred twenty hours to complete. That is twelve hours per song times ten songs. We knew we had to speed things up.

As time went on, we did speed things up. As we got more used to the recording process we got better and better. Our fifth song, *Power to Go*, only took us, on average, three takes each and the vocals only two takes.

Our ninth song, *Tough on Love*, we did first take for each of us except Rocks vocals. "Guys, we're getting good at this," I told them.

Killer was bouncing all over the place yacking about how quick our last song, and the album, would be done.

After we finished our tenth and final song, we were told the hard part is yet to come. Mark said, "next time we mix down guys, see you on Saturday," and shook our hands and we left.

When we got there on Saturday, Ritchie was there. "Hey, guys, how's my favorite band doing?" He asked us. "Clark says you guys are the bomb and after listening to the raw tapes, I got to agree," he told us. "Now's the time for the real fun," he continued.

"What do you mean?" Killer jumped up and spouted in his usual freaked out way. Ritchie said he meant we now get to listen and decide how each instrument and voice and drum hit sounds. He said this as he nodded at Killer. He went on to explain how we now would adjust each track to fit with each other.

"Each track was recorded as loud and as clear as could be. Now we adjust it to the way we want it to sound by itself and with the other tracks," he explained. "We need to make sure one track doesn't overpower another track, or all the tracks. This is also the time to decide if we need additional sounds, vocals and all, drums too Killer, added on to the recording. If you guys don't like your guitar sound on a song and want to redo it, this is the time we decide that, do you guys understand?" Killer again was bouncing all over.

"Killer, do you have any questions or suggestions?" Ritchie asked.

"Yes, I do," Killer blurted, "What if I need to add a ride hear or there?"

"This is the time we talk about those things and plan for them," Ritchie added, "We can add them tonight, but I'd rather us go through a song once first, get that one mixed, until you guys feel no more changes are needed and then move on to song two. So, let's listen to song one and see what you guys think."

We all agreed and listened through an incredible sound system I wished I had at home. We talked about the bass being a tweak to loud or Rocks guitar to soft or Killers high hat to loud and all of that and eventually got the sound to our liking. Unfortunately, that ended the evening for us. Mark told us he was pleased with the evenings work and said, "See you guy's next time, it's been great," and off we went.

Ah, home at last. We did get a tape of that one song, and I listened to it three or four times at least that night before Jennifer said, "Enough already honey, it's time for bed." She was right; after all it was two in the morning.

The next three weeks were cool, but tough. We did the same schedule but mostly listened instead of playing. We added stuff here or there. Killer did three high hat things on one song, on three separate tracks. We worked on two, maybe three nights per song. It was brutal. Sometimes one of us would ask if their part could be done over. "Yes, of course," Ritchie kept telling us, "Anything that sounds good to you guys," he would say, "any changes you need."

As with the recording process, the mix takes just as long and with more scrutiny. Now I'm beginning to see how it works. As the process continued, I watched Ritchie and Mark weave their sound magic. That's cool; I've got to remember that.

After we finished the album, sorry, the CD, we decided to have a party. Tin and Ginny threw it at their place. That CD played over and over again. It wasn't just the eight of us but Mark Clark and his wife Angelatiffa were also there. After dinner and lots of guitar playing, Mark says, "We have to start thinking about promoting this CD."

Killer comes right back in his usual bark manor, "How about promoting us?"

"Yes, that's what I mean guys," Mark continued, "The more CD's we sell, the more clubs we can play at, which means more dough, get it?" *Right on*, was our collective bark.

7

On Up the Road

After Mark Clark released our new CD to the local radio stations, and we started putting our name back out amongst the music club people, and found we were missed. It didn't take long at all till we were right back at the same old dives as well as some new and bigger places to jam in.

One of these gigs was a hush hush gig at Seubey's. The place, I'm glad to say, was packed. We played exactly what was on the CD and they loved us. How could we go wrong? As the next months went on, I realized the club managers, and Mark and his buddies, seemed a bit more energetic. Then one day he gathered us around and asked, "How would you guys like to play in Davenport?"

"Iowa?" I asked.

"Davenport, actually, is a growing city," Mark said.

"What's in Iowa that's not here," was the common question from all of us. The answer hit me stronger than the other guys, I guess. We can build from here and become bigger names. Sell the sound first and then go play the clubs. Mark continued on the idea that if we sell the sound, ahead of the band, we'd sell more seats at more shows.

"Sounds right guys?" I questioned.

"Let me explain this, guys," Mark continued, "Your CD has been selling like hot cakes in Iowa and even as far south as St. Louis."

"Are you telling us we could play almost anywhere?" Killer yelled enthusiastically.

Mark said, "yes, so to speak," as Killer bounced back to his seat.

"What do you mean?" Killer quietly asked.

"I've made some deals I hope you all will agree with." Mark told us. "I've made arraignments for two nights there in the Davenport area and two nights in the St. Louis area."

"You mean gigs?" I asked.

"Yes, what did you think I wanted you guys for?" Mark exclaimed. "Well, do you guys want the money or not?"

It turned out we played at two big clubs, one in Rock Island and one in Davenport. "Where the heck is Rock Island?" killer asked me.

"The Quad City's," I told him. "Let's go for this five-day ride and see where it takes us."

"Cool, man, cool," was Killers unusual calmness.

I jumped back in and said, "are you sure you want to go?"

"I do," he pounced, "But what about the girls, are they coming with us?" Yes, we all figured, cause how else would it work? I called Jennifer right away and she said she would see if she could take the time off work. She called back about ten minutes later all pumped up and proclaimed, "I'm ready to go to the Quad cities and St. Louis."

Later I asked the guys, "Jennifer and I are all set, what about you guys?"

"Let's go," was there response.

We all headed off for the long weekend, and it was fun. Win four nights, in three different cities. They loved us. After we got back, we talked and decided we could do this a lot more. The next thing I know, Mark calls and say's "Hey guys, uh dudes, I got us a line on Joplin, Kansas City, and Wichita, on the map for us. We're heading west," he told us.

I asked, "Kansas, or Missouri?"

"Well Kansas of course, I said we were heading west," he responded.

We did that weekend without the girls. That was tough. We did more of these weekend trips to other smaller cities around the mid west. Man, that was fun, although the girls only got to hang with us about half the time 'cause they were holding the real jobs. Yes, we had all stepped down from *real* jobs, but we had to do it.

All this time we had also been recording downtown. We made a second album, or as I was told again and again, *it's a CD dude*. We made our way all the way to Scottsdale, Arizona when I thought that maybe I could do a whole album, I mean CD, by myself. I don't know if I told you this or not, but in all of these years playing the bass, I've also learned how most stringed instruments work. I kind of squeak on the violin and can sort of blow some bad sounding horns. I also learned how to play a six-string guitar and keyboards, but not a big organ.

We cruised around the Midwest for a year or so when I decided I would do my own album, sorry, CD, you know, a solo thing. What did I know? I'd had my own songs brewing in my head for a while, so I decided, why not. I started by using the old stuff we had in the studio in Rock's basement. He kept asking, "Do you need a guitarist or anything?"

I just grunted "NO" and kept working. It took me three months or so till I got what I wanted. Now, what to do with it?

I played it for the guys and asked them what they thought. I said, "It would need a real drummer, but otherwise, what do you think?"

Killer had already been playing with his fingers and jumped up and said, "It's cool man, cool, do I get to play those drums?" Tin asked where this style or sound came from since I'd never shown this ambiance in my songs before. I explained that my own thoughts could never be the same as our combined thoughts.

"Wow, you're smarter than I thought you were," Killer laughs at me.

"Hey, thanks buddy, I didn't think you noticed," I chuckled back at him. Over all, they thought it was cool to play all of the instruments myself, except the electronic drums. Now on to our sound guy/great manager, Mark Clark.

I called Mark and said I was sending him a CD for him, and could I redo it in the old studio? After he heard it, he called. "Get up here as soon as you can, dude, 'cause you got something here." We set up a schedule for when we were both in town. It was all the time him or I could handle; after all we were now playing in Reno, Albuquerque and El Paso and pushing west.

By this time, we were hauling all our gear behind our old SUV's and pick-ups. We realized we had enough money to buy a big truck and haul it all together, so we did.

After four or five months of heading west, even into LA, Mark let us know that we had a gig in Atlanta waiting for us if we were interested. Well, I probably don't need to tell you, but we took it. My thoughts were, *next stop, the gardens.*

By the time we got around the country down to Atlanta, we had acquired a second truck with more equipment. After all, each new venue seemed to be bigger than the last.

Well, we finally made it east. We played Atlanta, Savannah, Charlotte, Richmond, and all the way up to Philadelphia and DC and north. Then we went west again to Pittsburgh and Cleveland, Cincinnati and Indianapolis, and on back home to Chicago.

The money was so good we added a third truck and a bus as an office. We also bought three more busses, which we divided up three ways. Jen and I and Rock and Lynn shared one, and Tin and Ginny shared with Killer and his current squeeze, Cori. We also had one bus for the crew, which we had to hire 'cause we had so much gear to haul around.

So, after our third tour around the country and hundreds of thousands of CD's sold, we rented a parcel of farmland with a farm-house on it and parked all the vehicles there and had a huge party.

While we were setting up a simple back yard jam space, I heard the phone ring and ran inside to get it. It was Mark Clark. "I know you guys just got back, but are you still coming up Saturday?"

"You're right, I kind of forgot. I'll see you Saturday." And back to the party I went.

An Old Introduction

When I got up the next morning, I checked my E-mail and had a Facebook request. It was from Katie somebody Bullard. Once I comprehended that it was Bullard's wife's Facebook page, I responded right away. Bullard's wife is from Wisconsin, and they were up there and heading south back to Florida in a few days or so. I E-mailed him and said I thought we should get together. I hadn't seen him since the army and hadn't talked to him in many years. His next E-mail said, *Sure, I was hoping you'd ask.* I gave them directions to the farm, and they stayed for a few days.

That first night we played acoustics and it was just Bullard and me. The next night all the boys were ready to jam. We played a lot of our stuff that Bullard liked, and we learned some of his tunes. The next night was Saturday and I told Bullard he's got to come up to the studio.

Mark was very impressed with Bullard and said he should join the band. Bullard thanked him and said, "I'd love to, but we have to get back home and back to our jobs." Before we left Mark's studio, Bullard and I decided we should record an album. Once Bullard had met Tinley and Rock he wanted to jam and record with all of us. How cool is that. We transferred music back and forth from here to Florida through the Internet and it came together pretty quickly. It's a good thing we both were using the same style of software. It only took a few weeks to put it all together and after Mark produced it and distributed it, it moved really fast. Three of the eight songs on the disc were hits. We hit it viral on the Internet after that and now everyone knows me. That's how I became a Rock Star.

"Yes, that's a great story Uncle Slate," my nephew exclaimed. His cousins yelled in agreement. I hope to see you all at our concerts and keep rockin'.

The End

If you have read this far, thank you. I believe some of you wonder who Slate Magma really is.

WELL

Okay, I'll tell you. I was born in Winnetka, Illinois and I went to New Trier East High School, class of '77.

Slate came from the mind of Brian J. Ewing

Thank You all for Reading my Book.

Printed in the United States
by Baker & Taylor Publisher Services